For Olivia, Suzanne, and John Keane
~ S. M.

For Norie – for all your hard work
in the background!
~ A. E.

tiger tales
5 River Road, Suite 128, Wilton, CT 06897
Published in the United States 2015
Originally published in Great Britain 2015
by Little Tiger Press
Text copyright © 2015 Steve Metzger
Illustrations copyright © 2015 Alison Edgson
ISBN-13: 978-1-58925-199-1
ISBN-10: 1-58925-199-7
Printed in China
LTP/1400/1155/0615
10 9 8 7 6 5 4 3 2 1

For more insight and activities,
visit us at www.tigertalesbooks.com

Waiting for Santa

by Steve Metzger

Illustrated by Alison Edgson

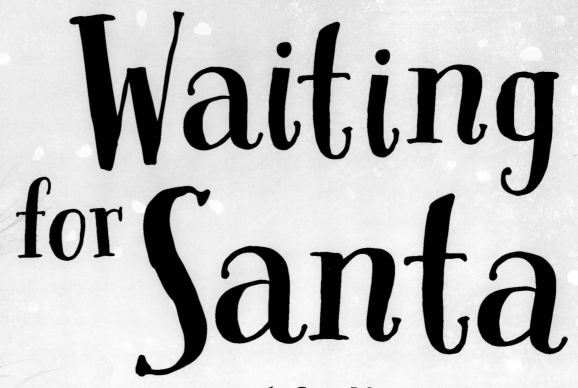

tiger tales

Bear woke early with a tingle in his tummy.
"Wake up, everybody!" he called. "Tomorrow's
Christmas! We've got to get ready for Santa Claus!"

"Santa's not coming!" Badger grumbled.
"He doesn't even know we're here!"

"He'll come!" Bear cried. "We just have to believe!"

"What's going on?" asked Mole. "Is Santa really coming?"

"Will there be presents?" squeaked Mouse.

"Stop this nonsense!" Badger said. "Santa's not coming this year . . . or *any* year!"

But Bear was hopping with excitement. "Santa will come!" he cheered. "He just needs some help to find us."

Bear's forest friends talked it over.
"Maybe he's right," said Hedgehog.
"Why don't we give it a try?" said
Mole and Mouse together.
"If we must!" huffed Badger.

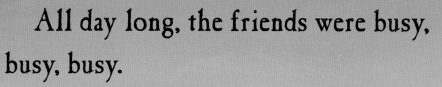

All day long, the friends were busy,
busy, busy.

"Santa will love our sign," Mole
said, "if he's here to read it."

"He'll be here!" Bear smiled.

"Santa's reindeer will love these snacks," Mouse said, "if they're here to eat them."

"They'll be here!" Bear declared.

"Santa will love our Christmas tree," Hedgehog said, "if he's here to see it."

"He'll be here! We just have to believe!" Bear exclaimed.

And he dashed off into the woods.

"Where's Bear off to now?" Mole asked.
"Maybe he's given up and gone home,"
Badger grumped. "Like *we* should!"

But Bear was back in an instant.

"Look at my Christmas star!" he cheered.

"I hope Santa will like it."

"But our tree is enormous!" Mole said.

"How will we reach the top?"

"We'll do it together!" Bear said.
He lifted up Badger, who lifted up
Mole, who lifted up Hedgehog,
who lifted up Mouse.

"I can't believe I'm doing this!"
Badger grumbled as they
wobbled and swayed.

Mouse stretched up high and tied the star to the tallest branch.

"Oooh!" she gasped, watching it sparkle.

"Ahhh!" sighed Mole in wonder.

"Eeek!" Badger giggled. "Mole, your feet are so tickly!"

"I can't help it!" chuckled Mole as they teetered and tottered.

And with a BUMP! they all fell to the ground.

Bear scrambled up. "Everything's perfect!" he said. "Now let's all wait for Santa."

So the friends huddled together as darkness fell.

"It's very cloudy," Hedgehog said. "What if Santa doesn't see our tree?"

"He'll see it," Bear said with a smile.

But the time passed slowly, and the wind began to whistle.

"I'm cold," Mole shivered. "I want to go home."

"Time for hot cocoa!" Hedgehog said, snuggling close.

But there was still no sign of Santa.

"He's not coming, is he?" cried Hedgehog.

"No presents?" sighed Mouse.

Maybe Santa isn't coming after all . . . .
Bear thought.

Suddenly, a big gust of wind blew the
clouds away. The moon shone down on the
Christmas star, making it shimmer and sparkle.

"There's something in the sky," Badger said.

"It's . . . it's . . . ."

"SANTA!" Mouse cried.
"And he has presents!
HOORAY!"

"Ho! Ho! Ho!" laughed Santa. "I could see that shiny star from way up high!"
There was a special gift for each of the friends.
"Thank you, Santa!" they said.
"No—thank you!" chuckled Santa.
"A rest and some yummy snacks were just what my tired reindeer needed."
"It's thanks to Bear," Badger said.
"He always knew you'd come!"

"What a wonderful welcome this is,"
said Santa, shaking Bear by the paw.
"A clever bear like you could help me
deliver these presents. Tell me, will
you come along?"

"Yes! Yes! YES!" Bear exclaimed. He hopped
into the sleigh and his friends all cheered.
And as they flew off into the night sky,
Bear and Santa called out together:

"Merry Christmas, everyone . . .
and NEVER stop believing!"

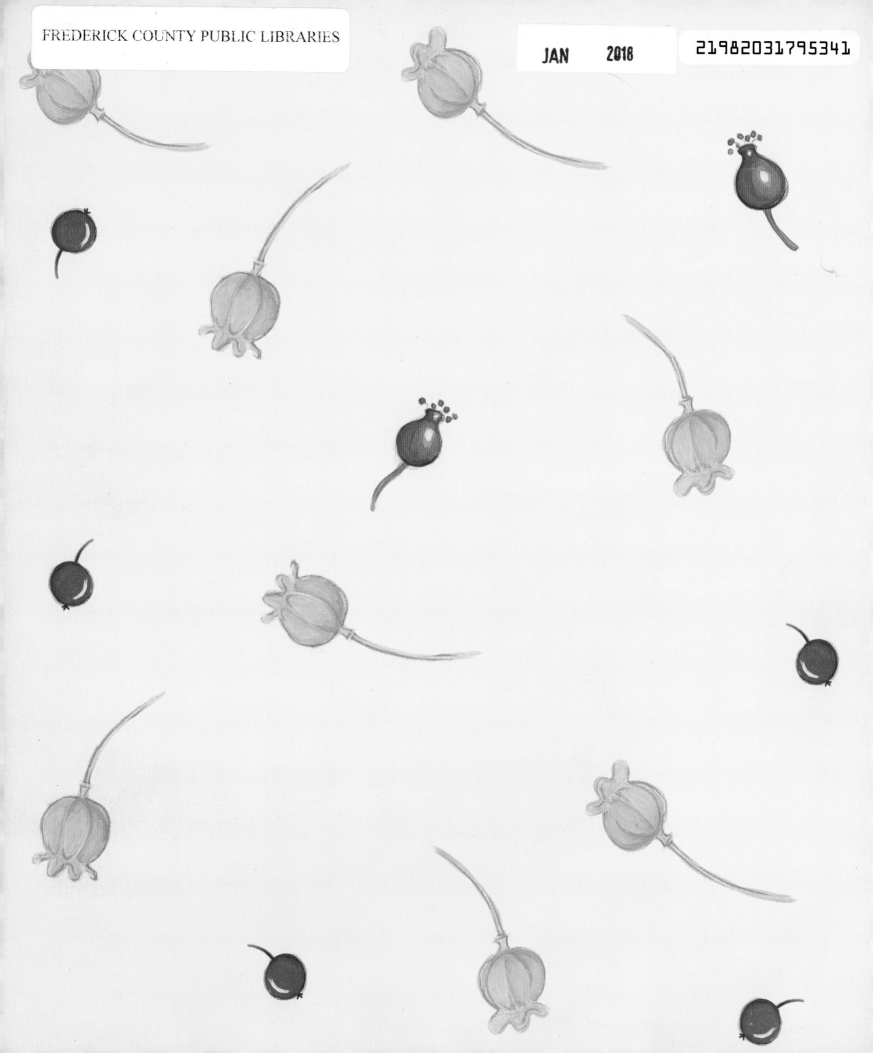